Super Hero

by:

E.C. Graham

Super Hero

For my three favorite super heroes
Will
Evan
& Chase

Written and illustrated by:
E.C. Graham

ISBN 978-1456463625

What is a super hero?

"True heroism is remarkably sober, very undramatic. It is not the urge to surpass all others at whatever cost, but the urge to serve others at whatever cost"
-Arthur Ashe

"We don't have to engage in grand, heroic actions to participate in the process of change. Small acts, when multiplied by millions of people, can transform the world."
-Howard Zinn

Like most boys his age Davey Davenport had his favorite toys and games to play.

Davey loved his toy wood building logs and used his favorite yellow dump truck to haul the logs around when building his magnificent creations.

However, Davey's favorite thing to play was Super Hero.

He imagined himself flying around town in his fancy costume and magic cape putting out fires and fighting crime.

He imagined people cheering for him and chanting his name.
He imagined being famous and loved by all!

One day Davey asked his mother if she would
make him a fancy super hero costume
with a magic cape.

"Of course I will Davey," said his mother, "but
just know that a magic cape and fancy costume
isn't what makes you a super hero.
It's what's within your heart that makes
a super hero super!"

Davey didn't know what his mother meant
by this, he was just happy that, at last, he was
going to have a super hero costume!

Davey was so happy that he wore his costume to school for show and tell career day.

"That's wonderful", Davey's teacher said "but remember, it's what's within your heart that makes a super hero super!"

Just then the bell rang for recess and Davey ran outside anxious to play super hero on the playground!

On the playground Davey noticed a group of kids picking on Wallace Washington. Wallace didn't have the coolest clothes and his shoe laces were often untied. He wore glasses, had freckles, and his hair was usually messy.

Davey was scared that his friends would make fun of him if he stood up for Wallace, but when he saw how sad Wallace looked he knew what he had to do.

Davey marched over to the group of kids, bent down to tie Wallace's shoe laces then put his arm around Wallace and said "come on friend, let's go play".

Wallace smiled and said "Thank you Davey. You showed me friendship when I needed it most. I hope someday I can repay you!"

At home, after finishing his homework, Davey ran down to his favorite spot at the creek behind his house to play. There he saw a beaver struggling to build a lodge for his family.

"What's the matter?" asked Davey.
"I can't find enough sticks to finish our house and my family will have no place to live" cried the beaver.
Davey knew exactly what he had to do. He ran back to his house and came back with his prized toy wood building logs.

"You would give me one of your favorite toys to use on my lodge?" exclaimed the beaver.
"Thank you", the beaver cried, "you sacrificed for me when I needed it most and I hope someday I can repay you!"

That night Davey lay awake thinking about the trip to the zoo he planned with his new friend Wallace.

As he lay awake he heard a bird in a tree outside his window that was unable to fly. Davey saw how sad the young bird looked and knew what he had to do.

"Walk along the tree branch to my window and I will fix your wing", Davey told the young bird.

Davey bandaged up the young bird's wing, gave him some food to eat, and made him a place to sleep in a drawer next to his bed. The next morning the little bird was flying around Davey's room.

"You fixed my wing", cried the bird as he flew out the window. "Thank you Davey. You showed me kindness when I needed it most and I hope someday I can repay you!"

At the zoo, the boys saw the lions, bears, and finally the elephants. Davey loved the elephants and when he leaned in to get a closer look he dropped his favorite toy dump truck into the elephant habitat.

The mommy elephant immediately stomped over and crushed Davey's truck.

When the mommy elephant saw Davey crying, she felt bad and said:

"I'm sorry, please forgive me. I thought your truck was a peanut. The sign that tells visitors not to feed us has been knocked over and now my baby is sick with a bellyache from eating the peanuts visitors throw at us!"

When Davey saw how sick the baby elephant was he knew what he had to do. He put the sign back up so all zoo visitors could see it.

"Thank you," cried the mommy elephant. "You showed me forgiveness when I needed it most and i hope someday I can repay you!"

Years went by and Davey grew up to have a house and family of his own.
One day at work Davey's boss told him the company was going out of business and soon Davey would not have a job.
Without a job Davey could no longer pay for his house or buy food for his family.
Sad and feeling defeated, Davey gathered his things and went home.

But, when Davey got home, he was further saddened to see that his home was on fire!
As the firefighters worked to put out the fire, word of Davey's sudden misfortune spread across town.
It spread to the beavers at the creek, the birds in the trees, the elephants at the zoo, and to the city where his old pal Wallace Washington worked.

When Davey's old friends the beaver, the bird, the elephant, and Wallace heard of Davey's misfortune they knew exactly what they needed to do.

"You showed me forgiveness when I needed it most", said the mommy elephant, "you are my hero. Now I will gather bricks and lumber to rebuild your house," and off she went.

"You showed me kindness when I needed it most," said the bird. "You are my hero. Now I will gather shingles to rebuild your roof," and off the little bird flew.

"You sacrificed for me when I needed it most," said the beaver. "You are my hero. I will use my tail to pack the mortar between the bricks and help rebuild your house," and away he went.

"You showed me friendship when I needed it most," said Wallace as he pulled up in a fancy limousine. "You are my hero. I would like to offer you a job with my company in the city!"

The animals worked hard and soon they had built Davey a beautiful new house.

Davey was overcome with gratitude. Surrounded by his childhood friends, he remembered the dream he once had to be a super hero.

His mother and teacher were right; he didn't need a fancy costume, a magic cape, or even fame to be a super hero.
It's what's within our hearts;
forgiveness, kindness, sacrifice and friendship, that makes a hero super!

There, surrounded by his friends and family in his beautiful new house, Davey finally realized what it meant to be a REAL super hero!

42346620R00017

Made in the USA
Lexington, KY
17 June 2015

What makes a super hero super?

Little Davey Davenport wants nothing more than to be a super hero when he grows up; so much so that he asks his mother to make him a super hero costume so he can practice. Follow little Davey as he goes on an adventure playing super hero, realizing along the way what it is that makes a super hero super!

ISBN 9781456463625

90000

9 781456 463625